Feliz Nawidog

THE STORY OF HOW SANTA'S DOG SAVED CHRISTMAS

By Reya & Ari Halper

Illustrated by Pencil Master Studio

To Shadow, our four-legged inspiration. And to children everywhere who never give up, even when nothing seems to be going your way.

Publisher's Cataloging-in-Publication Data

Names: Halper, Ari, author. | Halper, Reya, author. | Mehra, Priyam, illustrator.
Title: Feliz Navidog : how Santa's pet dog saved Christmas / by Ari and Reya Halper; illustrated by Priyam Mehra.
Description: Westport, CT: Sauce Idea Lab, 2020. | Summary: It is Christmas Eve and Pittsburgh is covered by a terrible fog. The only one who can save Christmas is Feliz Navidog.
Identifiers: LCCN: 2020905333 | ISBN: 978-1-7347854-0-1 (Hardcover) | 978-1-7347854-1-8 (pbk.) | 978-1-7347854-2-5 (ebook)
Subjects: LCSH Christmas--Juvenile fiction. | Dogs--Juvenile fiction. | Santa Claus--Juvenile fiction. | Pittsburgh (Pa.)--Juvenile fiction. | CYAC Christmas--Fiction. | Dogs--Fiction. | Santa Claus--Fiction. | Pittsburgh (Pa.)--Fiction. | BISAC JUVENILE FICTION / Holidays & Celebrations / Christmas & Advent | JUVENILE FICTION / Animals / Dogs | JUVENILE FICTION / Religious / Christian / Holidays & Celebration
Classification: LCC PZ7.1 .H335 Fel 2020 | DDC [E]--dc23

And Mrs. Claus, too, who helps spread tons of joy,
To each hopeful girl and to each eager boy.

There's Dasher and Dancer and Prancer and Vixen.

DASHER   DANCER   PRANCER   VIXEN

6

Comet and Cupid and Donder and Blitzen.

COMET CUPID DONDER BLITZEN

Then there're the elves, known to tinker away,
Making dolls, skateboards, and modeling clay.

8

Even of snowmen, we've all heard a ton.
Yes, we've heard every story, that is, except one:

About Santa's pet pooch, Feliz Navidog,
And the year he saved Christmas from Pittsburgh's worst fog.

'Twas the eve of the Eve, and just like they all should,
Santa's ole elves worked as fast as they could.
Ribbons were curled, and the presents were packed,
While Mrs. Claus made Santa's favorite snack.

The Nice List was checked, and, of course, then checked twice.
The flight plan laid out, as the sleigh got de-iced.

But just then, it seemed, Pittsburgh's fogginess grew!

And to make matters worse—

14

Everyone gasped at the thought of a flight,
Through the darkness and fog with no reindeer in sight.

"Christmas is Cancelled!" an elf cried to herself.
As everyone put the toys back on the shelf.

17

But Santa yelled, "Stop! This is not what we do.
Grab every last flashlight and a bucket of glue!"

So, ninety-nine flashlights they glued to the sleigh,
But it wasn't enough to light up Santa's way.

"What about flying?" asked an elf named Zeke. "I could build wings for the sleigh in a week!"

20

"Hold Christmas 'til New Year's? Now all hope is gone!
The kids would explode if they waited that long!"

21

They thought every thought they could possibly think
And wrote each of them down in blue juniper ink.
Yet, not one idea seemed to get the job done,
Though the Candy Cane Catapult sounded like fun!

Then Mrs. Claus felt an idea start to spark.
The furriest spark . . . in the form of a bark.
Yes, down at her feet and quite happy to help
Was Feliz Navidog, his paw raised with a yelp!

It was right then, when Zeke found a way through the fog: "Let's use sonar woofs from Feliz Navidog!

The sound waves will bounce off the objects ahead. We'll see clear as can be with barking instead."

24

Mrs. Claus looked at Santa, and Santa looked back
Their options were scarce to keep Christmas on track.
And while dogs and reindeer are not quite the same
It was try out Feliz, or go borrow a plane.

So, Zeke worked and he welded as fast as he could
On a sonar device made from stockings and wood.

26

Then they sprang into action, and in just one day
Trained Feliz Navidog how to fly with a sleigh.

But learning such things in a day is a feat,
It takes patience and focus and . . .

27

mountains of treats!

Then at last it was time for the moment of truth,
To see if his training was put to good use.
So, they all took a deep breath and, with fingers crossed,
Switched the sonar to "on" as the rein-dog took off!

29

He raced down the runway with paws everywhere.
And before Santa blinked, they were up in the air!

30

Woof! Woof! Woof! Navidog barked through the night,
Panting and soaring beneath the moonlight.

Ears flopping like windsocks and eyes wide as plates,
His first day as a deer was going quite great—

Although Feliz did chase a pigeon or two,
And sniffed Santa's butt while he tied up his shoe!

Then Southward they flew, hitting each little town,
As Santa scaled chimneys, going both up and down.

At last, they reached Pittsburgh; the fog was so thick,
Feliz barked so loudly, he nearly got sick.

But the presents each found their way under the tree,
While "Hos" filled the air up in large groups of three.
And no matter how foggy, no matter how dark,
Christmas stayed Christmas, all thanks to a bark.

So still to this day, you can hear, late at night,
Feliz Navidog, yapping proudly, midflight.
A part of the team, from that day until now,
Right there up in front, from New York to Moscow

36

A reminder that things often don't go to plan,
But think out of the box to turn can't into can!

37

The End

The Authors

Reya and Ari Halper are a father and daughter writing duo. A lot of fun, love, and laughter went into the creation of this book, and it greatly strengthened their bond. Hopefully this is something you will feel and see come alive on the pages that follow. It's also a backstory that we hope other kids and families will find inspiring, because FelizNavidog was truly Reya's idea.

As for a little bit more on each of us, Reya is eight years old and lives with her family in Westport, Connecticut. She is half Turkish, half American and 100 percent all about animals and creativity!

Ari is a writer by trade, coming from the advertising world. His work is some of the most famous and awarded in the industry. Highlights include fathering the E*TRADE Baby, creating a short film with Ron Howard called "When You Find Me," that shortlisted at the Oscars, and winning an Emmy for his work on Canon. Ari is slightly older than Reya.

Made in United States
North Haven, CT
06 October 2022

25117388R00024